The Tempest

Ariel
A spirit, Prospero's slave

Alonso
King of Naples

Gonzalo
A member of Alonso's court and Prospero's friend

Sebastian
Alonso's brother

Stephano
Alonso's butler

Trinculo
Alonso's court jester

Antonio
Prospero's brother who banished Prospero to the island

Prospero
The rightful duke of Milan

Miranda
Prospero's daughter

Ferdinand, prince of Naples
Alonso's son

Caliban
A savage, toad-like inhabitant of the island, Prospero's slave

C. A. Plaisted

Illustrated by Yaniv Shimony

QED Publishi

A ship in a storm

Act one

Out in the stormy sea, a ship was battling the waves. Its passengers trembled with fear. King Alonso of Naples was returning from a royal wedding with his noblemen. He was terrified that they would all drown. In such violent waves, his ship would surely sink. Nearby, however, there was an island. An island full of strange and magical things...

Twelve years earlier, Prospero, the duke of Milan, had been tricked by his brother, Antonio. He sent Prospero and his young daughter, Miranda, out to sea in a boat that he knew would leak.

Be not afraid, the isle is full of noises, sounds, and sweet airs, that give delight and hurt not
– Caliban

Antonio had hoped that the pair would not survive in the choppy seas. Antonio, you see, had wanted to be the duke of Milan himself. He had even persuaded King Alonso, a weak-willed man, to get involved in his plot.

Unknown to anyone however, Prospero and Miranda's ship had landed safely on the island. They had made a home for themselves, and their only companions for the past twelve years had been Caliban,

a savage, and a spirit called Ariel.

Prospero was a talented magician, who had spent a lot of time perfecting his magical powers. He had always preferred reading his books about magic to ruling Milan.

Prospero was also a loving father. His daughter, Miranda, had grown into a beautiful young woman – but with no one else her age for company, she was lonely.

Prospero watched the ship battling the storm and muttered magic spells under his breath. The wise magician had recognized King Alonso's flag on the ship immediately. He knew that his brother Antonio would be onboard and so had asked Ariel to help him conjure a mighty tempest.

Miranda rushed up to Prospero.

"Father! There's a ship and it looks like it's on fire! We have to help."

"Don't worry, my child," he said. "All is as it should be."

"I don't understand," Miranda said as thunder roared overhead. "Why don't you care? These people might be friendly."

Tell your piteous
heart there's
no harm done
– Prospero

Prospero knew better. Once he had thought Alonso was his friend, but he knew he could no longer trust him. This made him sad, for he knew that his old friend, Gonzalo, would be amongst Alonso's party. Prospero wished this kind and gentle man no harm. Prospero's feelings swayed from bitterness to forgiveness and back again.

"I'm afraid you don't know what some of those people did to us," Prospero sighed.

"It's because of them we are stuck on this island."

Miranda had only been a young child when they arrived on the island and her father had always refused to tell her about their past. Now a young woman, Miranda was finally ready to hear their story.

So, as the storm raged on, Prospero told his daughter about their background. Miranda hadn't known that her father had once been rich and important.

"It's my own fault," Prospero said, sighing. "I was more interested in magic than in governing. I let my brother run things for me.

Me, poor man –
my library was
dukedom large
enough
– *Prospero*

Little did I know that he was plotting to overthrow me."

Out on the ocean, the ship was being struck harder and harder by each wave. Engulfed in flames and hit by a final, crashing blow, it disappeared from the horizon.

"There are other ships out there too," Miranda gasped.

"But they aren't in the eye of the storm," Prospero said, grinning. "They'll make it back to Naples safely."

Miranda looked at Prospero, shocked. She'd never seen her gentle and loving father this beside himself. Knowing now that one of the ships and its crew were lost at sea, Miranda went back inside their home. Soon, her eyes began to droop. Her father had cast an enchantment upon her, sending her into a deep sleep.

Outside, Prospero watched the tempestuous sea. "Ariel!" he called. "What's happened to Alonso and his crew?"

Hast thou, spirit, perform'd to point the tempest that I bade thee?
– *Prospero*

8

"The king and his son, Ferdinand, have made it safely to our shore," the sprite explained.

Ariel knew that whilst Prospero had wanted to scare his foes, he meant no harm to any of Alonso's crew. Ariel had charmed the sailors to sleep through the storm. Safe from danger, their ship was floating, hidden from view. He would keep it concealed until Prospero decided its fate.

"Antonio and Sebastian, the king's brother, are also ashore," Ariel continued, "and so is Gonzalo."

"Very good. And where are they now?" Prospero asked.

"The rest of the fleet thinks Alonso and his men are dead. The other ships have returned to Naples," Ariel said.

"But we know that Alonso and the others are scrabbling up the rocks from the beach," Ariel added.

"Then my enemies are exactly where I want them to be," Prospero said. His plan was beginning to take shape.

"Ariel, I need your help with the castaways." Ariel looked at Prospero wearily. Prospero had been ordering him about ever since he set foot on the island and Ariel hated it.

"I'll help you, master," Ariel said. "But remember how you once promised to release me from my enslavement? Perhaps that could be my reward?"

Prospero sighed. "Bring me Ferdinand. If you help me this last time, I will free you!"

Do so, and after two days I will discharge thee
– Prospero

"Most gratefully," Ariel chirped and left in a flash.

Ferdinand was struggling to climb the rocks that led up from the shore in his wet clothes. Amongst the crashing waves, he had lost sight of his father and the rest of his crew. He feared they might all be dead.

"What is that?" Ferdinand whispered to himself. "Singing? I can hear singing! Who's there?"

Up above Ferdinand, hidden in a mist of invisibility, Ariel sang:

> "Follow me!
> Follow me
> this way!"

Unaware that a trick was being played
on him, Ferdinand followed. The song led
him straight to Prospero and Miranda.

Inside her room, Miranda also heard
the singing.

"What is it, father?" she asked as she
came out of her room. Prospero was sitting
by the fire when Ferdinand stumbled in.

"Who is that?" Miranda
asked, shocked.

"Who is this beauty?"
Ferdinand gasped when he
saw Miranda.

Miranda blushed.
During her many years on
the island, she had not seen
any man apart from her father. Now, as
handsome Ferdinand was walking towards
her, her heart leapt.

Prospero watched with satisfaction.
He knew that Ferdinand wouldn't be able
to resist his beautiful daughter.

"Come and join us for a meal,"
Prospero suggested.

Sitting next to each other at dinner,
Miranda and Ferdinand talked non-stop.
Neither of them had ever felt so happy
or relaxed. Prospero gave them delicious
things to eat and drink and soon the two
were filled with contentment both in their
stomachs and in their hearts.

Most sure, the
goddess on whom
these airs attend!
– *Ferdinand*

Prospero saw that Ferdinand and Miranda had fallen in love. His plan was working, but he wasn't going to tell them that. Instead, Prospero stood up and shouted at Ferdinand, "Leave my daughter alone!"

With a flash and crash of magic, Prospero conjured an invisible cage around Ferdinand, who suddenly found that he couldn't move.

"There," Prospero announced. "That's where you shall stay until I have decided what to do with you!"

"But father," Miranda protested, "why are you doing this?"

"Don't worry, Miranda," Ferdinand said from his cage as he reached for Miranda's hand. "As long as I can see you, I am happy..."

All washed up

Act two

Unknown to Ferdinand, other survivors were also swimming to shore. King Alonso was relieved to find his brother, Sebastian, had also made it to land. On the beach, they met with Prospero's brother Antonio, and Gonzalo, the honest old man who had been Prospero's friend. They gazed at each other in bewilderment, wondering how they had been washed ashore. Even stranger, their clothes were dry!

They had no idea that they were all caught up in Prospero's complex plot.

"Where is Ferdinand?" Alonso implored. "We must find my son!"

The men searched everywhere but couldn't find him. Eventually, they gave up.

"At least you have your own life," Gonzalo consoled the king.

"But my son is lost," Alonso whispered, hanging his head. "Please, leave me to my thoughts."

Beseech you, sir, be merry: you have cause – so have we all – of joy, for our escape
        – *Gonzalo*

"I am sure I saw him swim to shore," one of the crew added. Alonso was not convinced. Exhausted from battling the sea and from the grief in his heart, the king collapsed onto the beach.

Alonso's companions left him alone in his sorrow. Sitting further along the beach, they chatted quietly, wondering how they would be rescued from the island.

Ariel hovered high above them where he couldn't be seen. Desperate to earn his freedom, he began to sing again. Just as his singing had lured Ferdinand to Prospero's trap, so this new melody began to take hold of Alonso and his men. Within minutes, all but Alonso, Sebastian and Antonio were lulled into a deep sleep.

Seeing how exhausted their king was, Antonio said, "Sleep, dear king. Sebastian and I will stand guard for you."

Trusting his brother to care for him, the king slept.

What a strange drowsiness posesses them – Sebastian

"I know Alonso, Gonzalo and the others are tired from swimming ashore," Sebastian whispered, "but it's odd they are all sleeping this deeply."

"Perhaps it's the heat of the tropical storm," Antonio suggested.

As the others snored, the two men began to chat.

"If Ferdinand is dead," Antonio pondered, "then who will take over the throne when Alonso dies?"

Sebastian shrugged.

Antonio turned to Sebastian and said, "What if we were to kill Alonso? Then you could be king..."

Sebastian glared at him. "Kill my own brother?"

"With one stroke of

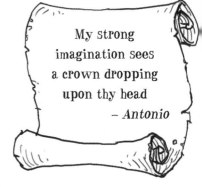

My strong imagination sees a crown dropping upon thy head
– Antonio

your sword it could be done," Antonio whispered. "I could help you. You would make a great king."

Sebastian began to imagine himself as the king of Naples... The more he thought about it, the more he liked the idea. He drew his sword.

"We could kill Gonzalo too!"
Antonio suggested, drawing his
own sword.

High above them, Ariel
was shocked. He began to
sing a different tune and,
one by one, the others
started to wake up.

"Why are your
swords drawn?"
Gonzalo asked drowsily.

"We heard a roar," Sebastian lied.
"It sounded like lions!"

"We must protect our king," Gonzalo
said, drawing his own sword.

"Come on – let's try to find Ferdinand,"
Alonso said, refreshed from his rest. "Lead
the way!"

That's right, thought
Ariel. Off you go to find
Ferdinand. Prospero would
be very pleased indeed!

So, king, go
safely on to seek
thy son
– Ariel

Far away on the other side of the island, the toad-like savage Caliban sat by his hut, grumpily building a fire. He had no idea there had been a shipwreck, or that his lonely world was about to be invaded...

Trinculo, Alonso's court fool, and Stephano, Alonso's butler, had lost the others and were looking for shelter. In doing so, they came across Caliban.

"What is this stinky thing?" Trinculo exclaimed. "He smells like a fish! And he's so ugly!"

"I need a drink just to look at him!" Stephano said, slurping from a bottle of wine that he had rescued from the sinking ship.

The two men teased and made fun of poor Caliban.

"Stop tormenting me!" Caliban said.

"He's short and stupid-looking!" Trinculo giggled.

"He's a monster!" Stephano shrieked.

Caliban cowered under his cloak. He hated his lonely life, but now he was afraid of these drunken louts and wanted to be left alone.

"Leave me!" he said again.

"Here," said Stephano, offering the wine bottle to Caliban. "Have a drink. It might make you less ugly!"

Open your mouth – here is that which will give language to you
– *Trinculo*

Mercy, mercy!
This is a devil,
and no monster
   – Stephano

Caliban refused, but Stephano placed the bottle at his lips and made him drink.

As he drank the liquid, Caliban's head began to whirl. He felt dizzy and confused. The liquor loosened his tongue and in no time the creature started to talk nonsense.

Stephano and Trinculo stood before him and laughed at his babbling. Confused, Caliban lunged towards Stephano.

"Are you a god?" Caliban exclaimed, so drunk that he could no longer see straight. "I should kiss your feet!"

"Come and kiss me!" Stephano teased.

"I will take you around the island," Caliban said, wobbling into a bow.

And so the unlikely trio set off to explore.

O brave monster –
lead the way!
   – Stephano

The tangled web unravels

Act three

The island was now full of activity. Alonso and his men were busy looking for Ferdinand while Caliban was on a drunken tour with his dubious companions. And, at the heart of the island, Ferdinand was doing Prospero's chores.

Prospero had released Ferdinand from his prison. He knew that the prince was so enchanted by Miranda that he would never run away. Prospero hid behind a bush to watch Ferdinand as he worked.

"I don't mind collecting firewood for Prospero," Ferdinand said to Miranda. "I will do anything for him if it means I can see you."

"But you shouldn't work so hard," Miranda said.

"I'm refreshed when I look at you," Ferdinand said, smiling and taking her hand. "You are the most beautiful girl I have ever seen."

Miranda blushed. "Do you love me?"

"With all my heart," Ferdinand answered.

Tears fell from Miranda's eyes.

"Why are you sad?" Ferdinand asked. "Miranda – will you marry me?"

Wiping her tears, Miranda smiled. "I'm crying because I'm so happy! Yes! I *will* marry you." The sweethearts embraced.

I am a fool to weep at what I am glad of
– Miranda

Still hiding, Prospero smiled as well. "At last some happiness has come out of this trouble," he whispered to himself.

Having drunk more wine, Stephano, Trinculo and Caliban were now staggering about.

"I am your slave!" Caliban burped.

"And my monster!" Stephano laughed.

High above, Ariel was itching to play a trick on them. He fooled them into starting a fight with each other. But they were so drunk they just collapsed in a heap.

"I am really Prospero's slave," Caliban said. "His beautiful daughter's, too. But I know how my master could be ruined."

Trinculo and Stephano sat up.

"Go on," said Stephano. "Tell us everything!"

"Prospero is a magnificent magician," Caliban explained, "but his books are his power. They have spells in them. Without them, he is worthless."

Stephano thought about this for a moment and then said, "We could kill Prospero. Then you would be free, and I could marry his daughter! That way I would have all his power!"

Trinculo laughed, while Caliban became quiet, regretting what he had said. From his hiding place above them, Ariel was shocked. He had to warn Prospero!

This will I tell my master
—Ariel

Back on the other side of the island,
Alonso, Sebastian and Antonio were
tired and hungry. They were still looking
for Ferdinand.

"Can you hear that?" Alonso asked.

Sweet music came sweeping across
the beach towards them. Out of the mist,
ethereal, almost-human shapes that had been
conjured by Prospero floated towards them.

"What are they?" Antonio gasped as
the shapes swirled around him.

"They're bringing us a feast!"
Gonzalo said.

All around them, the apparitions laid
out a tempting banquet. Starving, the men
sat down to eat the splendid food.
As they finished the last few mouthfuls,
bolts of lightning shot through the sky.

A curious creature appeared before
them. None of them had ever seen anything
like it before. Its head was that of an old,
angry woman with crooked, yellow teeth.

Its body was like a bird of prey's. The creature was a harpy. It shook its spiky, dark feathers as it strutted around them.

The harpy was actually Ariel in disguise. Prospero was watching the men from a hiding spot. Wanting Prospero to be pleased with him, Ariel clapped his harpy wings.

"You three are wicked men!" Ariel crowed at Alonso, Antonio and Sebastian. "You cast Prospero out of his home and sent him and his daughter out to sea!"

The men couldn't believe their ears. How did this harpy know their darkest secrets?

You fools! – I and my fellows are ministers of fate
– Ariel

"The storm was nature's punishment!" Ariel went on. "You've lost your son, Alonso, and all of you will carry guilt in your hearts forever!" With another clap of thunder, Ariel vanished.

Crouching in his hiding place, Prospero grinned at how Ariel had scared the three men. Now he had them all in his power! He giggled when he thought about them realizing that Ferdinand was very much alive and in love with his daughter!

O it is monstrous, monstrous!
– Alonso

As Prospero raced away, Alonso, Sebastian and Antonio shivered in fear. The other men of the party had not seen the harpy and now wondered what the three were talking about, especially as Alonso muttered Prospero's name. Gonzalo thought of his old friend, whom he had missed so much over the years. He noticed how guilty they looked. Perhaps this harpy was speaking the truth...

A lover's feast

Act four

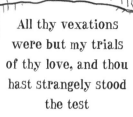

All thy vexations
were but my trials
of thy love, and thou
hast strangely stood
the test
– *Prospero*

Prospero returned to
Ferdinand and Miranda.
It was clear to him now
that they were genuinely in love.

"I've punished you enough, Ferdinand,"
he said. "I have seen how you feel about
my daughter and how much she loves you.
I give you my blessing to marry her."

Miranda's heart felt like it
would burst. She had
never dreamt that she
could be this happy.
Ferdinand clasped
her hand and
Prospero smiled.

"Go and
get ready," he
said. "We should
celebrate!"

Filled with happiness for the young couple,
Prospero conjured a group of sprites and
spirits to join them for the most splendid
of engagement feasts. As he watched the
celebrations, Prospero felt optimistic.
Maybe things were changing for good!

But then Ariel came and told him
about Trinculo, Stephano and Caliban
and their plot to kill him.

"Sprites! Spirits! Flee – our feasting is over!" Prospero commanded, angered at Caliban's betrayal.

"What's wrong with your father?" Ferdinand asked.

"I've never seen him this cross before," Miranda said.

With the other magical guests gone, Prospero turned to his daughter and future son-in-law.

"You must go and hide. I have some messy business to take care of," Prospero told Miranda and Ferdinand. When they had left, Prospero ordered Ariel, "Fetch Caliban and those other rascals."

"They'll be easy to find," Ariel explained. "I've tricked them into a confused state. I'll bring them to you now!"

With Ariel gone, Prospero set to work. He was going to teach Caliban a lesson. With great speed he conjured cloaks of velvet and silk, and lavish hats with frills and feathers.

Ariel was true to his word and quickly returned. He watched with Prospero as Caliban, Trinculo and Stephano stumbled towards the clothes Prospero had made appear.

Hiding behind the bushes, Prospero giggled at their stupidity.

"Look at these clothes!" Trinculo said. "They're fit for a king. Fit for King Stephano!"

"I'll have that gown!"
Stephano declared, grabbing
a velvet cloak from Trinculo.

"Leave the clothes alone,"
Caliban warned them.

"Oooo!" Stephano joked,
draping the cloak on Caliban. "Are you too
ugly to wear them?"

"Here, have this!" laughed Trinculo,
wrapping him in another cloak.

But Prospero had seen enough.

"Hounds!" he yelled, conjuring a
pack of spectral dogs to appear.
As they came into view,
howling, Prospero
shouted, "Chase
them!"

The terrified
drunken trio fled,
with the trail of
hounds snapping
at their heels.

Let them be hunted
soundly. At this hour
lies at my mercy all
mine enemies
– *Prospero*

From enemies, new friends are made

Act five

Prospero wrapped his magical cloak around him and thought about everything that had happened. He looked gratefully at Ariel.

"Sir, I think they have realized how badly they have treated you," Ariel said. "Alonso is broken from losing Ferdinand. Old Gonzalo is deeply saddened that everything has gone so wrong. Sebastian also wishes none of this had happened."

Prospero, too, had been through enough. "Bring them to me, Ariel," he said.

Then, Prospero stood up and drew a circle of magic around himself. He breathed in deeply and began preparing himself for the most powerful spell of his life.

Soon, Ariel returned with Prospero's enemies behind him. As they approached Prospero's magic circle of flames, they were terrified. Who was this powerful magician?

"So you don't recognize me?" Prospero asked. "Perhaps I should dress in my finery?"

Prospero changed into a fashionable cloak, fit for the duke of Milan.

If thou be'st Prospero, give us particulars of thy preservation
– Alonso

"Prospero!" Alonso gasped. "You're alive! Forgive me – I have been such a fool. And for my stupidity I have been punished most severely. I have lost my son."

Prospero glared at the king. After all Alonso had done to him, should he forgive him? But Prospero was tired of living a bitter and lonely life. He held out his arms to Alonso and the two men embraced.

"I, too, have lost my daughter," Prospero said, to test Alonso's remorse.

41

Alonso wept with guilt.

"Well then, now that I am back in my proper robes as duke of Milan maybe I can cheer you up, Alonso," Prospero said. He clapped his hands and called Miranda and Ferdinand from their hiding place.

"My son!" Alonso gasped as he wiped the tears from his eyes and embraced Ferdinand. "And who is this?"

"My dear Father, I'm so happy to see you are well! This is Miranda. We are engaged to be married."

"So they are our future king and queen of Naples," Gonzalo said happily.

"Give me your hands," Alonso exclaimed. "I am so happy to see you both."

The king turned to Prospero. "I'm not sure I understand all the strange things that have happened here, but I am truly sorry for how you have been treated. You are, of course, restored as the duke of Milan. Please forgive me."

Prospero looked at the king. "Let's not dwell on the past," Prospero said. He was glad to put all the bitterness and feuding behind him now that his rightful position was restored. "Come on – let's plan our future back in Naples."

Turning to Ariel, Prospero ordered him to bring back the king's flagship and its crew from its magical hiding place.

Oblivious to what had happened while they slept, Alonso's crew woke up and sailed to the island. As preparations were made to leave for Naples, Prospero asked Ariel to bring Caliban, Trinculo and Stephano back to him. They looked dishevelled and were still dressed in Prospero's robes.

I'll be wise hereafter, and seek for grace
– Caliban

"Forgive my foolishness, Prospero," Caliban begged. Now that he was sober, he was full of repentance.

"Isn't that my butler?" Alonso said, seeing Stephano.

This thing of darkness I acknowledge mine
– Prospero

"And my court fool, Trinculo? What are they wearing? They look a mess!"

"They have been drinking," Prospero said, sighing. "And they plotted to kill me."

Everyone turned towards Prospero.

Prospero looked at Caliban. He had never liked the creature, but after all these years, Prospero felt responsible for him.

"I have treated you poorly in the past," Prospero said. "Caliban, you are free. Go and live a quiet life on this island. After all, it is really your home."

"I will," Caliban said. Scared that Prospero might change his mind, Caliban fled to the far side of the island. He was finally free to live in peace!

Then Prospero turned to Ariel. "Tomorrow we will return to Naples. Will you promise us calm seas and strong winds for our journey?"

Ariel nodded.

"Then you are free," Prospero said.

Ariel smiled broadly. "Thank you!" he said and vanished.

Prospero watched happily as his former enemies laughed and chatted and his heart warmed to see his daughter so happy and in love.

"Let us plan a splendid wedding when we are back in Naples," Alonso declared.

The Duke of Milan grinned and nodded. "Let's start now. And let's celebrate our last night on this island with a feast."

As the others trailed off, Prospero touched his cloak and looked at his books. He remembered how his obsession with magic had led to him and Miranda being stranded on this island.

Prospero threw his cloak and his books into the sea and vowed never to do magic again. He had learned his lesson. Thanks to his new-found ability to forgive and the love in his heart, Prospero was finally able to let go of his bitterness and live a happy life at last.

The End

Now my charms are all o'erthrown, and what strength I have's mine own
– *Prospero*

Consultant: Dr Tamsin Theresa Badcoe
Editor: Alexandra Koken
Designer: Andrew Crowson

Copyright © QED Publishing 2012

First published in the UK in 2012 by
QED Publishing
A Quarto Group company
230 City Road
London EC1V 2TT

www.qed-publishing.co.uk

A catalogue record for this book is available from the British Library.

ISBN 978 1 84835 943 7

Printed in China